Ananse and the Lizard

For Chuku, who took me to Africa;
for Danny and Nell, who showed me their Ghana;
and for Nina, who went the distance
and inspired me to share what I found

Henry Holt and Company, LLC
Publishers since 1866
115 West 18th Street
New York, New York 10011
www.henryholt.com

Henry Holt is a registered trademark of Henry Holt and Company, LLC
Copyright © 2002 by Pat Cummings
All rights reserved.
Distributed in Canada by H. B. Fenn and Company Ltd.

Library of Congress Cataloging-in-Publication Data
Cummings, Pat.
Ananse and the lizard: a West African tale / retold and illustrated by Pat Cummings.
Summary: Ananse the spider thinks he will marry the daughter of the village chief,
but instead he is outsmarted by Lizard.
1. Anansi (Legendary character)—Legends. [1. Anansi (Legendary character)—Legends.
2. Folklore—Ghana.] I. Title.
PZ8.1.C895 An 2002   398.2'09667'0452544—dc21   2001001679
ISBN 0-8050-6476-1 / First Edition—2002
Typography by Martha Rago
The illustrations for this book were created with watercolor, gouache,
and color pencils on Fabriano Artistico hot-press paper.
Printed in the United States of America on acid-free paper. ∞
10 9 8 7 6 5 4 3 2

Ananse and the Lizard

A WEST AFRICAN TALE

retold and illustrated by

PAT CUMMINGS

Henry Holt and Company / New York

If you listen to stories during the day,
a bush will grow on your face.

IN GHANA, *where storytellers never want for*
an audience, this old saying is a warning to anyone
lazy enough to sit around telling tales while there is
work to be done.

But nighttime is another thing. When the moon is
full and the storyteller's every gesture can be clearly
seen, the tale springs to life.

Some of the favorite stories are about Ananse the
Spider: Ananse the clever, Ananse the greedy,
Ananse the trickster. His troublemaking is legendary.
But at times even Ananse's best schemes backfire.

So, if you lived in West Africa and you had finished
all your chores for the day, if you loved to listen to
stories, and if there happened to be a full moon, you
might just hear about Ananse and the Lizard . . . and
why lizards stretch their necks.

At the spot where a dusty road meets a rocky one, Ananse the Spider stopped to consider whether to head east or west when he saw a notice posted on a tree. "Well, well, well. What have we here?" he said, shifting the little bundle that held everything he owned.

"Hmmm." Ananse scratched his chin. "The Chief's daughter . . . someone will win her hand in marriage." Ananse chuckled to himself. If the Chief had to hang up notices to find a husband for his daughter, she must surely be a scrawny little thing.

Ananse read on, "'Whoever can guess her name . . .' How hard could that be? '. . . shall marry my daughter and win half my land and rule as Chief.'" Ananse read that line twice, then he scampered off to the west without bothering to read another word.

Now had Ananse read on, he would have seen the warning written at the bottom. He might have. But he didn't. And that is where the story begins.

Ananse found the Chief's village easily enough. Musicians were beating a *gong-gong* that could be heard for miles. Girls and young men crowded the streets, laughing and calling out to one another.

Ananse dodged the countless feet moving steadily in one direction. When he came to a high stone wall, he scurried up to get a better view. Ananse had just settled in a comfortable spot on a mango tree next to the wall when the *gong-gong* suddenly stopped.

"The Chief will be heard!" shouted a palace guard. Ananse found himself looking down into the courtyard of the village Chief. Three elegant women sat eyeing the crowd suspiciously. A line of boys gently waved large fans over their heads.

"The time has come for my daughter to marry," the Chief began. "Her name has never been spoken outside the palace. But whoever can guess her name will have proven himself worthy of marrying her and ruling half my kingdom."

Excited whispers raced through the crowd as all eligible young men pushed their way to the front.

"But," the Chief continued, "anyone who dares to come forth with the *wrong* name will have his head chopped off and fed to the buzzards!" The Chief nodded to a guard holding a large shiny blade, then marched back into his palace.

The crowd thinned out rapidly. Ananse dropped his sack to the ground and scrambled down from the tree.

"Do you mind!" said a lanky grasshopper. "Around here, we don't just drop things without looking first."

"One day," Ananse boasted, "you will tell your grandchildren that you were the first in your village to meet Chief Ananse. I might even invite you to the wedding." Ananse winked at Grasshopper. "Why, I may even find a place for you at the palace."

"Really?" Grasshopper grinned shyly. "I think I would like to live at the palace."

"Yes, well. . . ." Ananse reached for his sack. "I need a place to stay. Tomorrow will be a big day."

Grasshopper hugged Ananse's bundle tightly. "Please, friend, come have dinner at my humble home. I insist that you spend the night and allow me to prepare a feast for you in the morning . . . please?"

Ananse smiled. He let Grasshopper carry his sack and lead the way. His stomach growled, but Ananse knew it was nothing that a meal couldn't fix.

The dinner had only left Ananse more hungry. "Some meal," he grumbled. "Crumbs. Scraps. Twigs."

The minute Grasshopper dozed off, Ananse hurried back to the palace wall. A juicy mango would do what Grasshopper's dinner had not. Just as he reached for a nice ripe fruit, he heard voices and looked down.

"No one will come forward," one girl said.

"Only someone brave enough to risk his life," another teased.

"Or wise enough to learn your name," said the third.

"You'll see. Your father's test is clever, Ahoafé," added the fourth.

Ananse could not believe his luck. It was the Chief's daughter talking with her servants!

At that moment Ahoafé turned, and Ananse, stunned by her beauty, nearly fell from his perch.

"Ahoafé." He softly repeated the name over and over as he scurried back to Grasshopper's house.

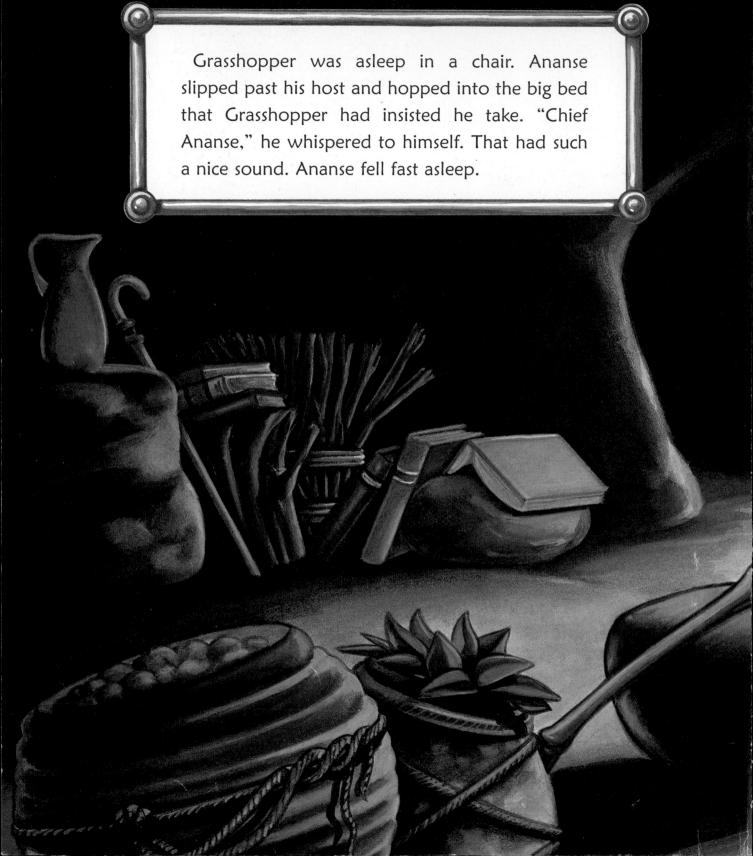

Grasshopper was asleep in a chair. Ananse slipped past his host and hopped into the big bed that Grasshopper had insisted he take. "Chief Ananse," he whispered to himself. That had such a nice sound. Ananse fell fast asleep.

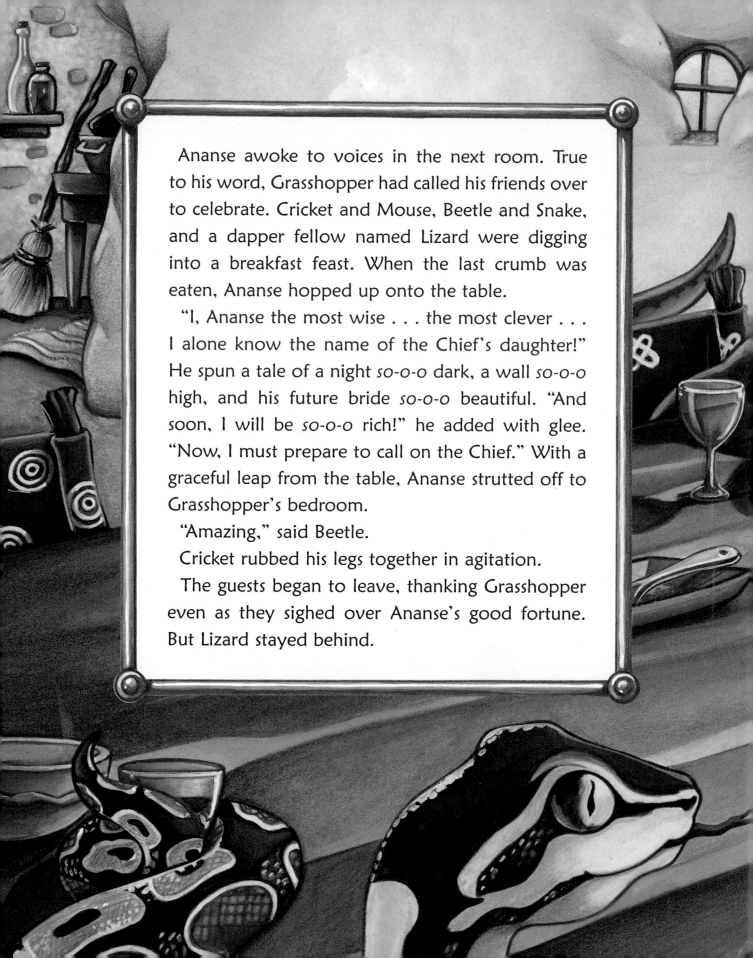

Ananse awoke to voices in the next room. True to his word, Grasshopper had called his friends over to celebrate. Cricket and Mouse, Beetle and Snake, and a dapper fellow named Lizard were digging into a breakfast feast. When the last crumb was eaten, Ananse hopped up onto the table.

"I, Ananse the most wise . . . the most clever . . . I alone know the name of the Chief's daughter!" He spun a tale of a night *so-o-o* dark, a wall *so-o-o* high, and his future bride *so-o-o* beautiful. "And soon, I will be *so-o-o* rich!" he added with glee. "Now, I must prepare to call on the Chief." With a graceful leap from the table, Ananse strutted off to Grasshopper's bedroom.

"Amazing," said Beetle.

Cricket rubbed his legs together in agitation.

The guests began to leave, thanking Grasshopper even as they sighed over Ananse's good fortune. But Lizard stayed behind.

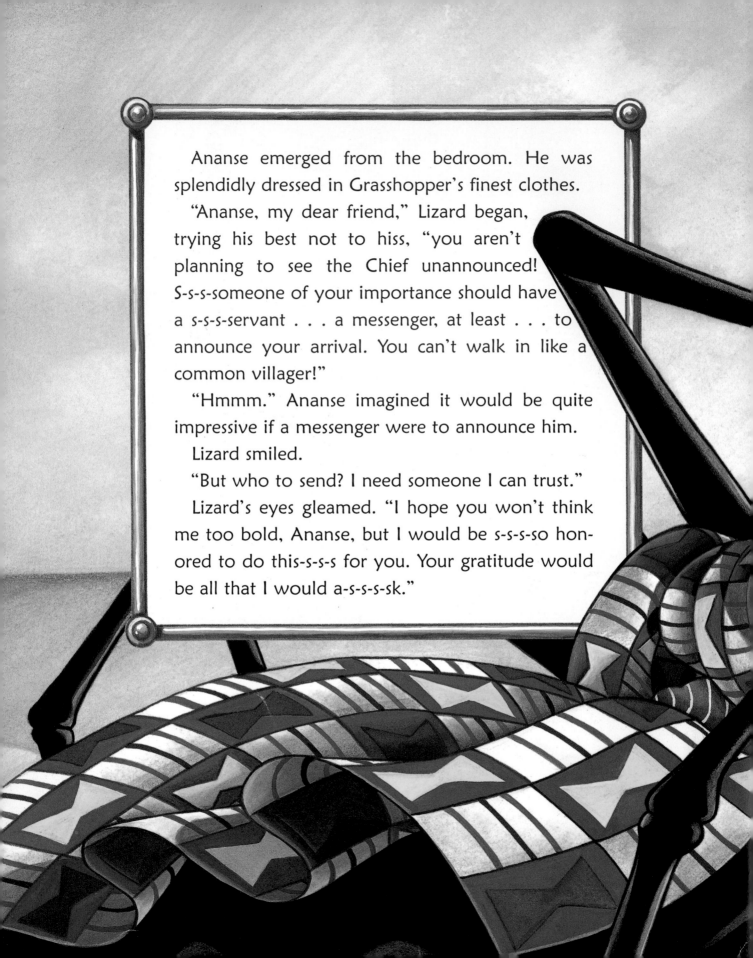

Ananse emerged from the bedroom. He was splendidly dressed in Grasshopper's finest clothes.

"Ananse, my dear friend," Lizard began, trying his best not to hiss, "you aren't planning to see the Chief unannounced! S-s-s-someone of your importance should have a s-s-s-servant . . . a messenger, at least . . . to announce your arrival. You can't walk in like a common villager!"

"Hmmm." Ananse imagined it would be quite impressive if a messenger were to announce him.

Lizard smiled.

"But who to send? I need someone I can trust."

Lizard's eyes gleamed. "I hope you won't think me too bold, Ananse, but I would be s-s-s-so honored to do this-s-s-s for you. Your gratitude would be all that I would a-s-s-s-sk."

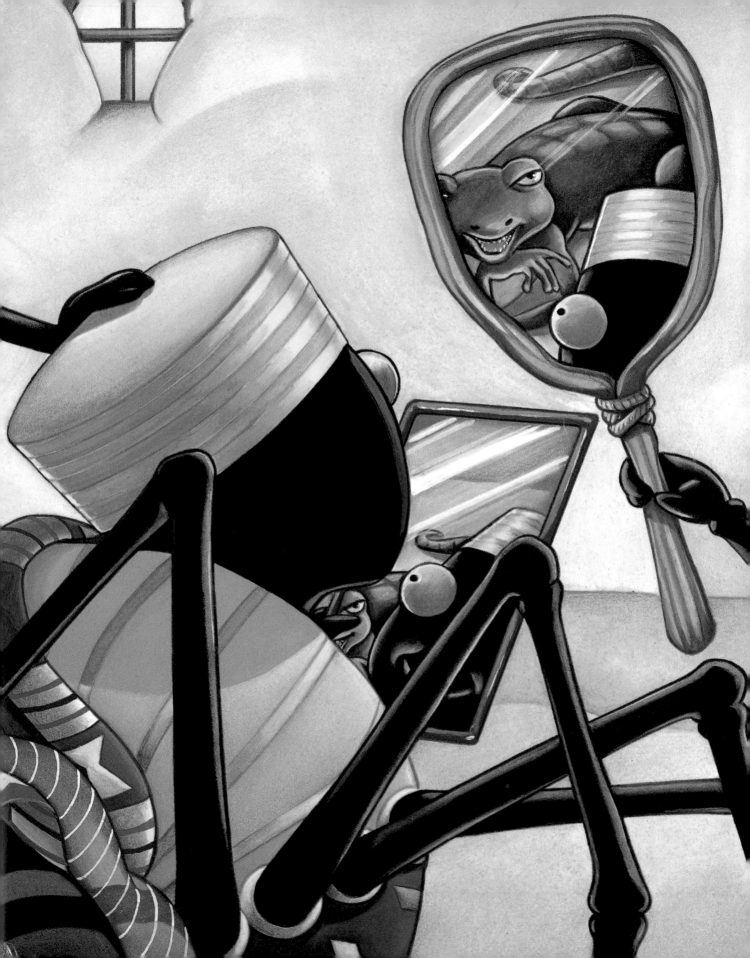

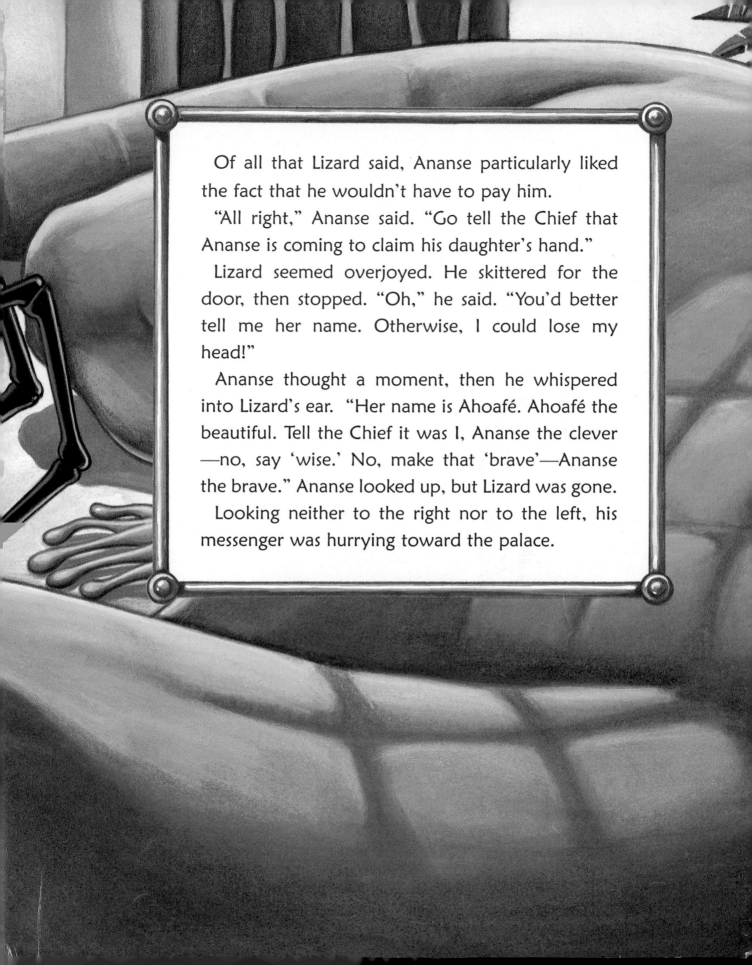

Of all that Lizard said, Ananse particularly liked the fact that he wouldn't have to pay him.

"All right," Ananse said. "Go tell the Chief that Ananse is coming to claim his daughter's hand."

Lizard seemed overjoyed. He skittered for the door, then stopped. "Oh," he said. "You'd better tell me her name. Otherwise, I could lose my head!"

Ananse thought a moment, then he whispered into Lizard's ear. "Her name is Ahoafé. Ahoafé the beautiful. Tell the Chief it was I, Ananse the clever —no, say 'wise.' No, make that 'brave'—Ananse the brave." Ananse looked up, but Lizard was gone.

Looking neither to the right nor to the left, his messenger was hurrying toward the palace.

Any lizard worth his tail can tell the story of what happened in that little village, on that wedding day, to that lucky lizard. As long as Ananse doesn't see him first, that is.

So if you look there, hiding in the corner, or there, scurrying along the wall, doesn't that lizard seem a bit nervous? Well, now you know why a lizard stretches its neck back and forth, back and forth, this way and that. Because long ago someone did warn Lizard.

◆ ◆ ◆